Mann
12 Bedford St.
NYC 10014

The Gingerbread Boy

ILLUSTRATED BY SCOTT COOK

Alfred A. Knopf · New York

This is a Borzoi Book published by Alfred A. Knopf, Inc.

Illustrations copyright © 1987 by Scott Cook
All rights reserved under International and Pan-American Copyright Conventions.
Published in the United States by Alfred A. Knopf, Inc., New York,
and simultaneously in Canada by Random House of Canada Limited, Toronto.
Distributed by Random House, Inc., New York.
Manufactured in Singapore
2 4 6 8 10 9 7 5 3 1

Library of Congress Cataloging-in-Publication Data
Gingerbread boy. The Gingerbread boy.
Summary: A gingerbread boy runs away from the woman who made him and from
several other creatures who wish to eat him, but a clever fox proves
his undoing.   [1. Fairy tales. 2. Folklore]   I. Cook, Scott, ill.   II. Title.
PZ8.G397Gh 1987 398.2'1 [E] 86-31278
ISBN 0-394-88698-4   ISBN 0-394-98698-9 (lib. bdg.)

To Anne and Denise

Once upon a time there was a little old woman and a little old man, and they lived alone in a little old house. They didn't have any little girls or any little boys at all. So one day the little old woman made a boy out of gingerbread, and she made a chocolate jacket with cinnamon seeds in it for buttons. His eyes were made of fine, fat currants; his mouth was made of rose-colored sugar; and he had a gay cap of orange sugar candy. When the little old woman had rolled him out and dressed him up and pinched his gingerbread shoes into shape, she put him in a pan. Then she put the pan in the oven and shut the door. Sitting there, she thought, "Now I shall have a little boy of my own."

When it was time for the Gingerbread Boy to be done, she opened the oven door and pulled out the pan. Out jumped the little Gingerbread Boy onto the floor and away he ran, out of the door and down the street! The little old woman and the little old man ran after him as fast as they could, but he just laughed and shouted:

"Run! run! as fast as you can!
You can't catch me, I'm the Gingerbread Man!"

And they couldn't catch him.

The little Gingerbread Boy ran on and on, until he came to a Cow by the roadside. "Stop, little Gingerbread Boy," said the Cow. "I want to eat you."

The little Gingerbread Boy laughed and said:

>"I have run away from a little old woman
>And a little old man,
>And I can run away from you, I can!"

And as the Cow chased him he looked over his shoulder and cried:

>"Run! run! as fast as you can!
>You can't catch me, I'm the Gingerbread Man!"

And the Cow couldn't catch him.

The little Gingerbread Boy ran on and on and on until he came to a
Horse in the pasture. "Please stop, little Gingerbread Boy," said the
Horse. "You look very good to eat."

But the little Gingerbread Boy laughed out loud. "Oho! Oho!" he
said.

> "I have run away from a little old woman,
> A little old man,
> A cow,
> And I can run away from you, I can!"

And as the Horse chased him he looked over his shoulder and cried:

"Run! run! as fast as you can!
You can't catch me, I'm the Gingerbread Man!"

And the Horse couldn't catch him.

By and by the little Gingerbread Boy came to a barn full of threshers. When the threshers smelled the Gingerbread Boy, they tried to pick him up. They said, "Don't run so fast, little Gingerbread Boy. You look very good to eat."

But the little Gingerbread Boy ran harder than ever, and as he ran he cried out:

> *"I have run away from a little old woman,*
> *A little old man,*
> *A cow,*
> *A horse,*
> *And I can run away from you, I can!"*

And when he found that he was ahead of the threshers, he turned and shouted back to them:

> *"Run! run! as fast as you can!*
> *You can't catch me, I'm the Gingerbread Man!"*

And the threshers couldn't catch him.

Then the little Gingerbread Boy ran faster than ever. He ran and ran until he came to a field full of mowers.

When the mowers saw how fine he looked, they ran after him, calling out, "Wait a bit! Wait a bit, little Gingerbread Boy, we wish to eat you!"

But the little Gingerbread Boy laughed harder than ever and ran like the wind. "Oho! Oho!" he said.

"I have run away from a little old woman,
A little old man,
A cow,
A horse,
A barn full of threshers,
And I can run away from you, I can!"

And when he found that he was ahead of the mowers, he turned and shouted back to them:

"Run! run! as fast as you can!
You can't catch me, I'm the Gingerbread Man!"

And the mowers couldn't catch him.

By this time the little Gingerbread Boy was so proud that he didn't think there was anybody at all who could catch him.

Pretty soon he saw a Fox coming across a field toward him. The Fox looked at the Gingerbread Boy and began to run.

But the little Gingerbread Boy shouted across to him: "You can't catch me!"

The Fox began to run faster, and as he ran the Gingerbread Boy chuckled:

> "I have run away from a little old woman,
> A little old man,
> A cow,
> A horse,
> A barn full of threshers,
> A field full of mowers,
> And I can run away from you, I can!

Run! run! as fast as you can!
You can't catch me, I'm the Gingerbread Man!''

"Why," said the Fox, "I would not catch you if I could.
I would not think of disturbing you."

Just then the little Gingerbread Boy came to a river. He could not swim across, but he wanted to keep running away from the Cow and the Horse and the people.

"Jump on my tail and I will take you across," said the Fox.

So the little Gingerbread Boy jumped on the Fox's tail, and the Fox swam into the river. When he was a little way from shore, he turned his head and said, "You are too heavy on my tail, little Gingerbread Boy; I fear I shall let you get wet. Jump on my back."

The little Gingerbread Boy jumped on his back.

A little farther out, the Fox said, "I am afraid the water will cover you there. Jump on my shoulder."

The little Gingerbread Boy jumped on his shoulder.

In the middle of the stream the Fox said, "Oh dear! Little Gingerbread Boy, my shoulder is sinking. Jump on my nose so that I can hold you out of the water."

So the little Gingerbread Boy jumped on his nose.

The minute the Fox got on shore, he gave a flick of his head and tossed the Gingerbread Boy high up in the air.

"Yap, snap!" went the Fox.

"Oh dear!" cried the Gingerbread Boy. "I'm one-quarter gone!"

"Gobble, gobble," went the Fox.

"Oh my!" cried the Gingerbread Boy. "I'm half gone!"

"Yum, yum," went the Fox.

"Oh no!" cried the Gingerbread Boy. "I'm three-quarters gone!"

"Mmmm!" went the Fox. But the Gingerbread Boy said nothing at all.
"All gone," said the Fox, licking his lips.